I0544188

a
cinderella
christmas carol
a suddenly cinderella series

a cinderella
christmas carol

a suddenly cinderella series

HOPE TARR

Entangled Publishing, LLC
10940 S Parker Rd
Suite 327
Parker, CO 80134
rights@entangledpublishing.com

Indulgence is an imprint of Entangled Publishing, LLC.

Edited by Alycia Tornetta and Stacy Abrams
Cover design by LJ Anderson
Cover photography by MaleWitch and PicsFive/Deposit Photos

Manufactured in the United States of America

First Edition November 2012

Chapter One

CHRISTMAS EVE, DECEMBER 24TH
UNION SQUARE, MANHATTAN, NEW YORK

"Happy Holidays, Ms. S."

Standing in her apartment building's marbled lobby, managing editor of *On Top* magazine Cynthia Starling—Starr—scowled at her doorman's grinning face. Even in the midst of pulling a double shift on Christmas Eve, Jimmie was so chock-full of holiday cheer it was almost sickening. Strike the almost—it *was* sickening.

He let the glass door fall gently closed behind her, his thin navy uniform scant protection against the raw, gusty evening. "Got big plans?" His eagle-eyed gaze rested pointedly on the plastic bag of takeout Thai food weighing down her left arm.

Starr swallowed a groan and settled for a noncommittal shrug. Doormen were notorious gossips, and a nice guy like Jimmie was no exception. She thought wistfully of her former Brooklyn Heights pre-war walkup with its creaking pipes, cracked plasterwork—and patina of privacy. Her current sleek new building boasted an onsite laundry room, gym, and a rooftop deck, not to mention its posh Union Square location, a mere ten-minute subway commute to the *On Top* offices. Still, at times such as this, she'd gladly sacrifice the luxury and convenience to be able to slip in and out without an audience.

Jimmie walked over to the kidney-shaped front desk, its glossy maple veneer buried beneath stacks of newly delivered parcels. "Before I forget, something came for you this morning."

"Great," she said, glancing down at her already full arms. Another holdup, just what she needed. Would this day—this *holiday*—never end?

Jimmie darted behind the desk. Burrowing through the piles, he brought out a medium-size box covered in plain brown packing paper and handed it to her. "Hope it's just what you asked Santa for."

Santa—oh, puh-lease! "Yeah, whatever, it's probably a work thing, but thanks."

Her gaze zoned in on the return address, and she snatched it, pulse picking up. Although there was no name, the Washington, D.C., address gave her a pretty good idea of the sender.

Macie Freakin' Graham!

She hadn't spoken to her former features editor since Macie had gone rogue on her that autumn, falling for the subject of her undercover investigation—famous radio personality Ross Mannon—and quitting not only the story but also the magazine, right in the middle of Starr's staff meeting, no less. That Mannon had once done his damnedest to take down the magazine was apparently forgiven and forgotten in the hormone rush that Macie's month-long masquerade as his housekeeper must have released.

So much for five years of grooming! So much for

gratitude! If it hadn't been for Starr, Macie would still be writing engagement announcements for her hometown newspaper. At the very least, Macie might have given her a heads-up on the whole quitting thing. Still, a part of Starr—the squishy soft part she worked really hard to hide—wasn't only professionally put out but personally hurt. Over the course of five years of shared Fine Wine Fridays and Sushi Saturdays at *On Top*, plus the occasional movie and drinks meet-up outside of work, she'd thought she and Macie had become more than just boss and employee, that on some level they were...*friends*.

Lesson learned.

So far she'd refused to reply to the wedding invitation along with Macie's other overtures—e-mails, texts, and even a few sad-sounding voice messages. If Graham—make that Graham-*Mannon*—thought she could soften her up with some bullshit holiday peace offering, she was about to learn otherwise. Still, being human meant being, on some level, curious. She'd take the box up to her apartment, allow herself a quick peek inside, and then give it to Jimmie with instructions to ship it back.

"Thanks." She tucked the parcel beneath her arm and turned to go.

Jimmie's voice stalled her. "Look, Ms. S., I was just wondering if you maybe don't have plans for tomorrow"—once again his gaze slid down to the takeout bag knocking against her knee—"maybe you'd like to join me and my family at the homeless shelter for women and kids in Astor Place. They put on a big Christmas spread every year. My wife and kids help with serving the food, and I dress up as Santa. We've been going every Christmas Day for five years now, and I wouldn't miss it. If you could see the smiles on those little kids' faces when..."

He bleated on, but Starr tuned him out. If Jimmie wanted

to spend his day off stuffed inside a Santa suit, that was his business, but Starr considered holiday-inspired volunteerism a crock. Being charitable one day a year might make do-gooders like Jimmie feel all soft and gooey inside, but people needed to eat three hundred and sixty-five days a year, not only on December twenty-fifth.

Aiming her gaze at the bank of elevators, one of which was out of order yet again, she shook her head. "I have other plans, but thanks."

It wasn't, strictly speaking, a lie. She did have plans—plans to spend the holiday home alone with her cat—but that didn't mean Jimmie's was her only invitation. There had been another—from the magazine's new art director, Matt Landry.

With his sexy half smile, washboard abs hinted at beneath his T-shirts, and hazel eyes that shifted from mostly blue to mostly green with mesmerizing swiftness, Landry was too hot for her to manage as she did the other members of her team and too damned good at his job for her to do anything other than get out of his way. Being anywhere in his vicinity turned her insides to Jell-O and other parts of her to the scalding liquid mocha lava cake they'd featured in December's food column. The degree to which she'd noticed him, every nuance of him, from that very first interview seven months earlier had alarmed her. It *still* alarmed her. At thirty-four—okay, soon-to-be thirty-five—she was too old to indulge in an office crush, but also sufficiently senior that she couldn't risk letting it become anything more. And then there was the issue of their not-exactly-insignificant age gap. Landry might have the aura of an old soul, but his smoking hot body had walked the earth for just twenty-eight years.

For a guy still in his twenties who'd spent most of that time in his native Florida, he'd amassed an impressive portfolio. Even the low-profile catalogue and hotel brochure stuff had blown her away with its unique vision and edgy creativity.

His was a high-energy vibe that *On Top* needed to tap into. To live up to the boast of its name, the magazine needed more than a new logo. It needed a fresh vision, an artistic voice that would resonate with its Generation-Y readership. Leafing through his book, Starr had quietly conceded that Matthew Gabriel Landry was the very best candidate for the job. She couldn't exactly justify not hiring him simply because she didn't trust herself around him. Time was money and interviewing candidates took up both. Besides, a stud like Landry probably had a harem of twenty-something twits on the hook. She'd figured on being more or less invisible to him as a woman.

She'd figured wrong.

That evening, while cramming papers into her laptop case in preparation for leaving, she'd had the sudden disconcerting sense of being watched. She'd looked up—and found Landry standing in her open office doorway, his intense hazel eyes stroking over her, the shifting sands of his irises caressing her face. The times when he showed up unexpectedly, and her guard was down and her will weak, the brilliance of his beauty seemed to burn her aquamarine eyes to ash and drain the last drop of moisture from her mouth.

"What is it, Landry?" she'd snapped, and immediately felt the hot sting of a blush strike her cheeks, her redhead's porcelain complexion, as always, a dead giveaway.

He'd hesitated, the fluorescent hallway lights haloing his shoulder-length hair—the wavy chestnut locks freed from his customary work ponytail. "A group of us is going for drinks. You know, chill out and celebrate tomorrow being a holiday. I—*we*—were wondering if you might want to come with."

She'd shoved a copper-colored curl out of her eyes and let out a brittle laugh to cover her heart's wild drumming. "And risk being lynched? I don't think so. Thanks but no thanks."

It might be Christmas week but the magazine world

had already moved on to Valentine's. As the month of hearts and flowers, February was their single biggest seller of subscriptions and generator of ad revenue. It was also scarily behind schedule, and with Macie's replacement yet to be found, Starr was seriously short-staffed on the editorial side. To make up the missed time, she'd told her entire team, including Landry, to be back in the office on December twenty-sixth. She'd never been exactly popular with her people, but the tough decision to curtail Christmas vacations had hefted the bar toward hate.

The December holiday-themed issue had come out weeks ago. She mentally ticked off the article titles and taglines. *Cuddling up on Christmas Eve, Latest Lingerie Trends and Mistletoe Must-Haves, What to Wear (and NOT to Wear) to Sleigh Him on New Year's Eve*, and, of course, the latest reworked take on what was pretty much every month's anchor story: sex. *Hanukkah Hankie Panky and Christmas Canoodling: Seven Sexy Secrets to Have Him Ho-Ho-Hoing in the Sack*. Imagining canoodling with Landry beneath a brightly lit Christmas tree—the silken feel of his taut, Florida-tanned flesh bared and rippling beneath her fingertips, her wearing skimpy scarlet lingerie and five fewer pounds—shot a quiver of desire through her.

"The way you're smiling, Ms. S., you must be planning on some serious celebrating for sure."

Snapped back to attention, Starr spied the knowing smile on Jimmie's face and felt hers flame. "My plans aren't anyone's business."

Like a bum Christmas tree bulb, Jimmie's smile flickered to blackout. "Sorry about that, Ms. S. You have a good hol—*time* whatever you do."

Eager to escape, she marched over to the working elevator and jabbed the button. Tapping her foot as the floor numbers dipped downward with maddening slowness, she silently ticked off her to-do list. Most of the action items had been taken care of earlier, if not altogether crossed off. Still, the sense of having let something slip nagged at her. The elevator landed—finally!—and the double doors pulled back. She stepped swiftly inside and pressed the fifth floor and close buttons before anyone could join her. Not that there were many people left around. The one upside to Christmas was it emptied out the building. By now, more than half of her fellow residents would have left the city for somewhere else, somewhere they identified as "home." The laundry room, gym, and elevator would be more or less hers until Sunday night.

Watching the elevator climb to her floor, she couldn't wait to get inside her apartment. Christmas Day might be a load of crap—it *was* a load of crap—but it was still a day off. A day to read, to marathon watch all the TV she missed during the week, and to chill out with her Maine Coon cat, Molly Jane. Hers might not be a storybook existence, but at least she was living in reality, not some glittery Christmas Fools' Paradise.

But the biggest reason of all for spending the holiday alone, the reason for the single Crumbs cupcake tucked inside the top of her takeout bag, was that tomorrow wasn't *only* Christmas Day. Crappy Christmas was also her crappy birthday, her *thirty-fifth*.

Yes, Virginia, there was a Santa Claus—and in Starr's case the Jolly Old Elf had pulled double duty as Santa Stork.

Chapter Two

Balancing her burdens, Starr stooped to fit the apartment key into her deadbolt lock. A familiar braying meow greeted her even before the door opened. She stepped inside to find Molly Jane waiting in her usual spot, black ears and fluffy black tail sticking straight up. As always, the sight of that beloved little fur face had her spirits lifting and her heart softening.

She put down her bags, shrugged out of her coat, and reached down to stroke the silken black head. "How's Mommy's good girl? Hungry, I'll bet."

The black-and-white tuxedo cat meowed loudly and leapt to meet her outstretched hand, demanding more. It was hard to believe the kitten she'd rescued a few days after 9/11 was a senior now. Closing in on twelve, Molly Jane didn't act her age or otherwise seem aware of it. Blissful oblivion to birthdays, what Starr wouldn't give for that!

Straightening, she hung her coat up on the hooked mirror, kicked off her heavy boots, and carried the plastic bags inside the galley-style kitchen, a slender space outfitted with state-of-the-art appliances, tall maple-finished cabinets, and black marble countertops. She cracked open a can of Science Diet, forked the contents into a clean cat bowl, and set it down on the tiled floor. "Bon appétit, baby."

The cat's head dropped to the bowl like an anchor, and Starr looked lovingly on as the tuna-flavored pet food quickly became history. Since Macie's leaving, Molly Jane was unabashedly Starr's best friend. Who was she kidding? With Graham permanently out of the picture, her pet was her *only* friend.

Reaching down for the empty bowl, the nagging sensation of having forgotten something returned. Silently she mentally ticked off her list again. Drop off the dry cleaning, including the angora sweater with the red wine stain—the winter *white* sweater, wouldn't you know?—check. Remind her assistant editor, Terri, to finalize the February ads with the magazine's advertising department—check. Email Landry about the revised logo design for the new cover concept—check. Call her mother in Arizona, thank her for the early birthday card, and wish her and Husband #2 a good Christmas? Distasteful as it was, she'd done that duty, too.

She glanced down at the receipt stapled to the outside of the carryout bag and suddenly it hit her. She'd forgotten to stop at the ATM. No wonder Jimmie had talked off her ear. He'd probably hoped she'd come around to remembering his Christmas bonus before he got off shift.

Another problem with living in a big fancy high-rise was that the staff always had its hand out, especially at Christmastime. Along with giving Jimmie his end-of-year bonus, she was expected to tip the rest of the building crew. It added up. It wasn't like these people didn't get salaries and, in the case of the super, his apartment was included as a perk. Jimmie, however, lived in Astoria, not far from the blue-collar neighborhood where Starr had grown up. He and his wife had a bunch of kids, including their youngest son,

Timothy, born with some sort of crippling scoliosis.

Unfortunately, picking up the few grocery staples from the bodega and then the cupcake and takeout food had brought her down to seven dollars, not counting any coins that might be buried at the bottom of her purse. And her bank's ATM was on the opposite side of Union Square. For a few fleeting seconds she considered putting her coat on and heading back out but quickly squelched the thought. Screw it! She would give Jimmie and the others their bonuses some time before New Year's. Sure, Jimmie could probably use the extra money *for* Christmas but that wasn't really her problem, was it? It wasn't like she'd *asked* him to have such a big family or to fritter away what funds he had feeding false hope to homeless kids.

She grabbed the food along with a cold Corona from the fridge and Macie's box and headed out into the living room, devoid of holiday decoration like the rest of the apartment. Landing on the sectional sofa, she set everything down on the coffee table except for the gift. Molly Jane hopped onto the cushion beside her and head-butted the box as if urging Starr to open it.

Starr gave the gift a good shake, and then used her keys to tear through the heavy brown paper. Lifting the oblong latched box lid, she saw an envelope lay atop a bed of Christmas red tissue paper. She broke the seal and slid the card out.

The printed front read, "Thinking of You on Your Christmas Birthday." *This ought to be good.* Inside bore a handwritten message:

Dear Starr, the note began.

Dear, my ass. Stuff it, Graham.

I know we didn't exactly part on the best of terms…

Talk about an understatement.

…but I wanted you to know that I still remember your

birthday, along with all the other mostly great times we shared during my five years at On Top. *Your present was first worn by a famous film actress in the 1930s. Legend has it that it brings the wearer luck in love. I'm still trying to figure out whether or not I believe in luck, let alone legends, but if there is any luck or, better yet, magic in these, I figured what better time than Christmas to pass it on and who better to pass it to than you, Boss Lady.*

Happy Christmas Birthday from your former features editor and always friend,

Macie

So Graham had sent her something wearable and apparently vintage. Now that she was sleeping with the enemy, money must be no object. Curiosity piqued, Starr dropped the card on the coffee table and returned her attention to the custom box, antique with rosewood inlay. She felt around the velvet-draped lining and took out the first tissue-wrapped item. A shoe! Unwinding it from the paper, she sucked back a breath. The crimson-covered velvet evening shoe was from Saks Fifth Avenue—*vintage* Saks Fifth Avenue. She took out the mate and examined it as well. A rhinestone was missing, but otherwise it was in the same pristine condition—no distinct signs of damage or cracks in the leather. Starr hesitated. Resolved as she was to return them, the shoes were too special not to at least try on.

She slipped on the right shoe. Given the high arch and narrow toe, she'd expected it to pinch, but instead her foot sank into the rich velvet as though it were a vat of butter. She put on the second, and then leaned forward to buckle both ankle straps. Feet propped on the edge of the glass-top coffee table, she sat back and admired the effect.

She'd never before thought of her feet as dainty, but

silhouetted by the rich red velvet, they looked it. The tiny amber topaz rhinestones caught the light, winking up at her like tiny stars, or maybe even the Bethlehem Star after which she was nicknamed. The shoes were so exquisitely unique she was half tempted to keep them. But no, she didn't accept gifts, not for her birthday, not for Christmas, and certainly not for the sake of a backstabber looking to ease her conscience at the holidays. She carefully unbuckled each shoe, rewrapped them in the tissue paper, and put them back in the box.

"Better to have loved and lost," she said, closing the box and sliding it beneath the table.

Hungry, she broke open the containers of lukewarm Thai food, snapped apart the set of wooden chopsticks, and dug in. Molly Jane sniffed appreciatively, pink nose working, and head butted Starr's hand.

"Sorry sweetie, no people food for you," she said, moving a container out of range.

Shoveling up Shrimp Pad Thai, Starr stretched out her free hand for the TV remote. Surfing the channels yielded one crap Christmas program after another. From animated children's classics like *Rudolph the Red-Nosed Reindeer* to Christian choirs and choral groups to evening services broadcast from notable churches and cathedrals, there was no escaping. Even her trusty standby, the classic film channel, had caved, showing a black-and-white version of *A Christmas Carol*.

Yawning, she popped open the beer and sat back to watch for a while. Cynic though she was, she couldn't help feeling sorry for Scrooge. From where she sat, he wasn't so much a villain as a Type A personality trying to get his shit done. He had also probably really, *really* needed to get laid. Starr could relate.

Her thoughts circled back to Landry. Recalling the way his jeans clung to his trim waist, hugging his slender hips just so, made her mouth water. She eyed the Crumbs cupcake set out along with the other food containers and licked her lips. Visible inside its clear plastic container, it was as yet untouched. Screw sticking in the candle and making some stupid wish that wasn't going to come true. Screw delaying gratification until her birthday's official start. Screw it, or better yet, *humbug* on it all. She snapped open the plastic lid, lifted out the icing-drenched confection, peeled away the waxed paper wrapper, and bit in.

So...freakin'...good.

The first big sloppy bite was followed by another and another. The birthday cupcake was quickly gone. Sucking frosting from her thumb, she glanced back at the TV, where one of the visiting ghosts—a large bearded Bacchus-like take on Father Christmas—gorged on his conjured Christmas feast while two rail-thin child spirits, "Ignorance" and "Want," looked forlornly on.

Starr took a swig of beer. "Fabulous, now I can be thirty-five *and* fat."

Midnight and her Christmas birthday were fast approaching. She usually stayed up to toast it, but this year she wasn't so sure she'd make it. Not sure at all. Maybe it was the tryptophan from the chicken satay or the recent combination of too many early mornings and late nights, but suddenly she couldn't seem to hold her eyes open.

Onscreen, Scrooge had taken hold of the spirit's robe as directed and was being flown over a snow-sheathed London skyline. The actor playing Scrooge put on an impressive performance of looking cold. Starr didn't have to act. The temperature outside must have dropped dramatically because the apartment felt as though, like Bob Cratchit, she was making do with a single lump of coal.

She shivered and hugged herself. "For this I pay four grand a month."

Too tired to get up and go to bed, she reached for the throw blanket, pulled it over her, and stretched out across the couch cushions, Molly Jane burrowing against her. She slipped off to sleep just as the bell of nearby Grace Church struck the first of twelve chimes—midnight.

Chapter Three

"Psst, Starr, wake up."

Starr cracked open an eye and then quickly closed it again. What was Matt Landry doing in her apartment in the middle of the night? And was he...*glowing*?

I am so dreaming.

Even though she hadn't spoken, Matt's voice answered her. "No, you're not. Open your eyes and look at me."

Though used to giving orders, not taking them, Starr complied. She opened her eyes—and bolted upright. Landry squatted beside her sofa. His handsome face wore the same expression of unflappable patience she'd seen in staff meetings when she was being a particular bitch.

He lifted a brow. "I don't think you're a bitch. You're just...very clear on your goals."

"Jesus, how do you do that?"

He smiled. "You're easier to read than you might think. All I have to do is look into your eyes. They're the windows to the soul, you know."

He'd said almost the exact words to her at work last week

when they'd crossed paths in the break room—on purpose, or at least it had been on her part. Like the Pied Piper, he'd been too irresistible not to follow, even if she'd done so on the pretense of refilling her water bottle.

She fitted a hand across her forehead. "If I'm awake, if we're *really* having this conversation, then you're a visual and auditory hallucination. I repeat, visual *and* auditory. Not winning!"

He chuckled. "That bad, huh?"

"It means I'm bat shit crazy, schizophrenic at the very least. Thanks but no thanks. I'll take dreaming over a life lived on antipsychotics any day. Good night." She made a grab for the cover.

His hand shot out, pulling it back. "If I'm a dream figure or a hallucination, then I wouldn't feel solid, would I?"

Starr hesitated. Before now, she'd never considered what the rules might be. "I…guess not."

He held out his hand palm up. Like the rest of him, it was rimmed in a gently pulsing white light. "Touch me."

She hesitated. If only he knew how she'd ached to do just that ever since he'd started at *On Top*—then again, if he could read her mind, no doubt he *did* know. Suddenly being schizophrenic seemed the better bargain. Dodging his gaze, she gingerly stretched out her hand and wrapped it about his bigger one.

"Holy shit."

He was flesh and blood, warm and solid, so solid that she could detect the hint of calluses rimming the inside of his knuckles. Vaguely she recalled from reading his résumé that, before moving to New York, he'd worked on old cars. The factoid had been listed at the end under "Interests and Hobbies." Before Landry, she'd never bothered reading that far.

She pulled away. "Who are you? *What* are you? And

what have you done with Matt?"

Growing up as a latchkey kid, she'd had the Sci-Fi Channel as her babysitter and *Invasion of the Body Snatchers* as her favorite cult classic film. Still, even with her child's imagination, the prospect of alien life had seemed a farfetched fantasy—until now.

"I'm Matt, or at least an aspect of him. For tonight, think of me as your Spirit of Christmas Past, Present, and Future."

"I hate to sound like a stickler, but aren't those supposed to be three separate spirits?"

A faint frown creased his handsome face. "Well, technically, yes, but this is a very busy time of year. Besides, haven't you heard? There's a recession on," he added with a wink. No doubt about it, he had Landry's trademark humor and unflappable charm down pat.

"You look like Landry, only more…shimmery," she admitted.

Even blinged out in a glittering silver-sequined three-piece suit that the late Liberace would have coveted, he looked pretty freakin' fabulous. Still, the Landry she knew was strictly a jeans and T-shirt guy.

He frowned. "The Powers That Be fashioned me in the form they knew you would be most receptive to."

Starr didn't have a comeback to that. Privately she acknowledged that The Powers That Be must be pretty smart cookies.

Matt surveyed the coffee table littered with half-finished takeout containers and shook his head. "Holed up at home, alone, eating greasy Thai take-out when you could have been out enjoying yourself with friends."

Despite their bizarre situation, Starr bristled. Just because he'd styled himself as some sort of…Christmas ghost guide didn't mean he got to barge into her life and criticize it. "First, that Thai food isn't greasy. It's some of the best in the city, much more nutritious than the fried pub grub I would have ended up eating had I gone along for drinks. Second, I don't have friends."

He leaned in. "Are you so sure about that?"

Starr caught her breath. He dazzled her and not because of the glowworm thing. *Get a freakin' grip, Starling. Repeat: this is not the real Matt, this is not the real Matt, this is not the real Matt...*

"Besides, they didn't really want me there. You—Matt—just asked me along to be...nice."

For a few seconds, he looked as though he might argue. Instead he stood and stretched out his hand to her again. "Come on, we have a packed schedule of Christmases to power through and not a lot of time."

Starr groaned. Packed schedules, deadlines—even in her delusions, she couldn't catch a break. "Jesus, Casper, what gives? Do you turn into a pumpkin? Did The Powers That Be give you a curfew—be back by dawn or no wings for you?"

"Wings are for angels. You've mixed up your Christmas classics. You're thinking of *It's a Wonderful Life.*"

"My bad," she admitted. "But spirits or angels, what does it matter? Neither exists."

He rolled his glowing eyes, and despite the shadows, Starr could make out the distinct green and gold flecks. Just as with the real Matt, staring into his eyes made her feel all...melty.

He shook his head, sending his loose chestnut-colored hair billowing like a cloud. "You're not about to make this easy on me, are you? Why does that not surprise me?"

"Okay, I'll humor you and go. Only what am I supposed to call you?"

"Call me?" He sent her a puzzled look.

"Yeah, 'Ghost' sounds kind of generic. And you've already suggested you're not so keen on Casper. Can I call you Matt? Since you're kind of borrowing his body and voice for the night, it seems only fair."

"Sure, you can call me Matt, but not Landry. He really hates that, by the way."

Starr was sincerely surprised. "He does? He's never said anything. I call everyone on my team by their last name."

"I know you do. It's one of the many tactics you use for keeping other people at a distance."

She snorted. "Well, excuse me, Dr. Freud."

Ignoring the interruption, he continued. "He's hoping you'll give it up in time and come around to not only calling him by his first name but letting him into your life."

Landry—Matt—wanted into her life? This was news. Her pants maybe, but her life was a tall order. Still, the possibility that he might see her as more than his boss or a quick no-strings-attached office fling was…intriguing. Starr had hoped to let the subject drop, but Spirit Matt persisted. "He asked you out tonight, didn't he?"

She forced a shrug. "A bunch of people were grabbing drinks after work, that's it. It wasn't like you—I mean, he was asking me out on an actual date."

Again that telltale brow lifted. "Are you so sure about that?"

Starr hesitated. Was she? If she'd given in and gone out with them, might the casual group meet-up have segued to a real date? She'd never know now.

"Take my hand and whatever you do, don't let go."

Starr barely had time to wrap her hand around his wrist before their feet left the ground. The apartment floor-to-ceiling glass window blew open despite her having secured it earlier. As if entering a wind tunnel, they were sucked through.

Batting curls out of her eyes with her free hand, a terrifying thought—even more terrifying than being levitated and now flown several hundred feet above ground—seized her. "The window…my cat…if she jumps up on the sill, she could fall out."

"Don't worry, I closed it." As in their real, at work lives, he seemed to not only think of everything but take care of it, too.

She let out a relieved breath and dared a look down. The Manhattan skyline stretched out beneath them like a glittering urban Christmas canopy. Far removed from the din of car horns and ambulance sirens and cursing cabbies, the silent city seemed serenely, surreally beautiful. Although she'd been born and raised here, Starr felt as if she were seeing New York for the first time through fresh, gentler eyes. Caught up, it took her a few minutes before realizing they were leaving the city behind.

"Where are you taking me?" she called over the rushing wind.

Matt kept his gaze straight ahead—a good thing, she guessed, since he was, technically, "driving" them. "You'll see soon enough."

The East River came into view. They headed toward and then over it. Starr spotted the Triborough Bridge and suddenly she *knew*. "You're taking me to Queens, aren't you?"

He didn't deny it.

They set down at Astoria Boulevard. Above them, the N Train powered past. Having grown up less than a block away, Starr remembered the bone-rattling rumble all too well.

"That was one smooth landing," she said, shaking snow from her hair. Despite being dusted with the stuff, she felt pleasantly warm.

He smiled. "Thanks, I'll pass on the compliment to The Powers That Be."

"Please do. While you're at it, remind me to fill out the comment card," she joked.

Dream or delusion, she might as well have fun with it. She couldn't remember the last time she'd felt so light or carefree, the last time she'd allowed herself to let go and have a real… adventure.

"Will do." His expression sobered. "Compliments lift everyone's spirits, especially when they're sincerely meant. If you spent half as much time praising your team members as you do tearing them down, the results might surprise you— pleasantly."

Starr stiffened. Just when she was beginning to loosen up and enjoy her dream—delusion, whatever it was—he had to get all preachy. "Whipping a magazine team into shape is a lot like training in the military—sometimes you have to break people down before you can build them back up again, better and stronger."

His glowing gaze dimmed. "Suit yourself." Turning away, he started walking. Afraid he might decide to leave her there, sans Metro card or money—or shoes, for that matter—Starr started after him.

"Hey, wait up. Don't be pissed off. I mean, it's my management style, that's all. It's not personal."

"Maybe it should be," he said softly, gliding across the slippery snow-banked street with ease. Then again, his feet didn't exactly touch the ground.

Gingerly following a few steps behind, she opened her mouth to answer when a familiar sight stopped her in her tracks. "Oh my God, is that what I think it is?"

He halted. "Yes, your first home."

The charred-colored brick building looked exactly like the apartment house where she'd spent most of her childhood. "But they bulldozed it years ago."

"I know."

"Then how—"

A wave of dizziness washed over her, causing her to leave

the thought unfinished. She blinked against the sudden head rush. Opening her eyes, she saw they no longer stood outside the building but within it—in the kitchen of her former fifth floor walkup.

Crossing the linoleum, she reached out and touched the peeling gold-brown wallpaper with gentle fingers. "This is... amazing," she said.

And it was. From the grease-splattered cabinets to the buckled tile to the aroma of garlic and frying onions wafting through the vent from the apartment below, everything looked and even smelled exactly as she remembered.

The rent-controlled studio apartment had been the best her single mother could afford, small for even just two people, although given her mom's schedule of racing from one low-paying part-time job to the next, it wasn't like she'd logged in enough at-home time for Starr to feel crowded. What she had felt was lonely. Even a studio space felt big and empty when you were the only one in it. Library books, magazines recovered from the recycling bin, and the trusty TV had been her windows to a larger, brighter world—brighter, or so she'd thought.

"How did you manage to...recreate all this?" she asked.

He beckoned her to follow him farther inside. "I didn't recreate anything. These are all your memories. They live inside you always. Come and see for yourself." They entered the main room to the iconic introduction to Rod Serling's *The Twilight Zone.*

You unlock this door with the key of imagination. Beyond it is another dimension...

Starr mouthed the words, following along with the announcer. Having grown up watching reruns of the original black-and-white sci-fi/fantasy series, now a cult classic, she knew the introduction by heart and had seen most of the episodes countless times.

A land of shadow and substance...

Once relegated to her fantasies of space and time travel, those words suddenly felt strangely prophetic, fitting.

Caught up, it took her a moment to notice that the apartment wasn't as empty as she'd first thought. A red-haired child in pink PJ's sat cross-legged on a blanket spread over the uncarpeted floor, her back to them and her attention riveted on the flickering TV screen.

Starr crept closer so as not to startle her. A few steps in, understanding struck. "Oh my God, she's me!"

Flanking her side, Matt nodded. "On the Christmas you turned ten." He strolled over to the old-fashioned radio alarm clock set on a rusted snack tray, the room's only table. "Looks like you have another seven and a half minutes to go."

A jingle of keys announced the apartment door opening. A red-haired woman in a shapeless coat stepped inside, her arms weighted with bags and her weary young face wreathed by a big smile. "Merry Christmas Birthday!"

Starr turned toward her, a lump lodging in her throat. "Mom?"

The Spirit touched her arm. "She can't see or hear you. She's only a shadow. They both are."

"And yet they—we—look so...real."

Child Starr whipped around. "Mommy!" she cried out, aquamarine eyes shining. The TV forgotten, she shot to her feet and flew across the room. Heedless of her mother's full arms, she hugged her hard. "I thought you had to work all night. I didn't think you were coming." Between her mother's day job at the deli and moonlighting nights at the 24/7 diner, they hadn't had much time together.

Her mother's roughened hand stroked Child Starr's curls. "I told them I needed to take off early, that Christmas is my baby's birthday."

Child Starr lifted her head and looked up. "It's almost

midnight."

Her mother took a step back. "In that case we'd better get cracking. We've got a tree to decorate and a birthday pie to cut."

"It was Boston Crème," Starr said aloud, remembering. "She couldn't afford to buy a birthday cake, but her boss let her bring home one of the day-old pies so I would have... something."

Standing beside her, Spirit Matt laid a warm hand atop her shoulder. "It looks to me like you had quite a lot."

"Yeah, I guess maybe I did," she admitted, watching the scene.

"What tree?" Child Starr asked, her puzzled gaze searching the room.

"Ta da!" Her mom held out one of her bags, a burlap-bagged spruce, the tree so tiny and misshapen it was little more than a twig. "I was lucky, the tree seller gave it to me for free. It was his last one left, and he wanted to go home and be with his family. What do you think?"

Child Starr stared at the tree, her face falling, and Adult Starr remembered struggling with her disappointment. She'd seen the big, beautiful trees for sale earlier in the week, and her mom's little tree in no way measured up. "It kinda looks like the Charlie Brown Christmas tree," she finally answered, biting her bottom lip.

Her mother propped the tree against the wall and put down the other bags beside it. Still wearing her coat, she turned back to Child Starr and dropped to her knees so that they were on eye-level. "Starr, sweetie, not everything is measured by how much it does or doesn't cost. It's the love we put into things—into each other—that matters the most. That's what Christmas is all about. That's why I call you Starr, after the star that guided the Wise Men to Bethlehem. You give my life purpose, baby girl. You're my reason for going on."

Child Starr's mouth curved into a smile. "Beats Cynthia, I guess."

Her mother let out a laugh and reached to ruffle Child Starr's curls. "Naming you Cynthia was, I'll admit, your father's idea."

"Too bad he didn't bother sticking around for the baptism," Adult Starr said, fending off the familiar stab of pain.

She'd grown up believing her father had died in an accident. It wasn't until she was a teenager that she'd learned the truth; he hadn't wanted to be a husband or a dad. He'd split a few months after Starr was born, leaving her mom holding the proverbial bag—and the baby.

As yet blissfully ignorant of that family fact, Child Starr only smiled. "I'm glad you came home, Mommy."

"So am I, Starry Girl, so am I. But I don't want you to ever worry. No matter how late I have to work, I'll always come home to you, promise."

Eyes damp, Starr watched as the salvaged tree was summarily set in its stand and the diner leftovers spread out on the blanket along with plastic forks and paper plates. Her mother punched ten slender pink wax candles into the pie's wilting whipped cream topping, lit them with her Bic disposable lighter, and sang "Happy Birthday" in her endearingly tone-deaf voice. Child Starr made a wish and blew out the candles, all ten, and they devoured big sloppy pieces of melted, slightly stale pie that, Starr remembered, had tasted delicious. Afterward, late though it was, mother and child busied themselves with stringing popcorn and hanging handmade craft paper ornaments on the tree.

"Poor in pocket, rich in love," the Spirit's voice broke in, startling her.

Eyes filling, she turned away from the cozy tableau.

"Mom could always spin shit into gold. She still can. She has a knack for making something out of nothing."

Except when it came to men. By the next year, her mother would have met and married Jeff, AKA Loser Husband Number One. Along with monopolizing her mother, Jeff took over their apartment, including the TV remote, as though he owned it—pretty ironic considering he stayed jobless for most of the six-year marriage. *Twilight Zone* episodes were few and far between. So were smiles. Listening to him burping back beer and cursing from the couch hadn't made for a very happy Christmas birthday. Eventually Starr had stopped celebrating it, and Christmas, altogether.

Spirit Matt lifted a dark eyebrow and studied her with his inscrutable hazel gaze. "You're a lot like her."

Caught off guard, she whirled on him. "I am *nothing* like my mother."

Getting knocked up while still in high school, working for pittance wages and putting up with rich people's crap, going through men like they were facial tissue—her mother's path wasn't one she'd ever wanted to walk down. From an early age, Starr had made certain she set her course for a very different life, focusing on books and not boys, taking shit from no one, and making sure she made the grades to earn a scholarship to NYU's journalism program.

Rather than argue, the spirit said, "It's time to move on." He held out his hand.

Still miffed, she stared at the offered hand as though it were a snake before relenting and taking it. "Let me guess, assuming we're staying at all on script, the second whistle stop on this Christmas Train would be—"

"Christmas Present."

Chapter Four

They were back in Manhattan, in the East Village, standing outside of Central Bar. Unlike Astoria, still buried beneath sludge from the latest snowstorm, here the streets and sidewalks were pristinely salted and swept.

Emotionally raw from the recent visit to Christmas Past, Starr turned to Spirit Matt. "A bar, seriously? If you wanted a drink, I have beer in the fridge at home. As it is, I'm feeling a little underdressed, not to mention I'm pretty sure there's a no-bare-feet rule for patrons. Join me or not, it's up to you."

She turned toward Fourth Avenue. Fortunately, the Irish pub–styled watering hole was only a few short blocks' walk from her Union Square apartment. He caught her arm. Though his grip was light, he held her in place with no apparent effort. Starr hoisted her head, intending to tell him to go to Hell. Instead she froze, spellbound. Even draped in the silly sparkling suit, the Matt before her was one hunk of human spirit. Drinking in the beauty of his sculpted features, basking in the intensity of his glowing gaze, she wondered what it would feel like to have the real Matt hold her as his spirit form was so masterfully managing. Giving herself a mental shake, she reminded herself that as his boss, she couldn't afford to find out. Dating a subordinate wouldn't get her fired, but it could be the death knell to a future promotion. Like her visits to Christmas Past and now Present, any thought of a future with Matt Landry was best left to her dreams.

"Remember," Spirit Matt was saying, "no one can see us. Besides, I didn't bring you here to drink. I brought you here to show you something—someone." Dropping his hand from her arm, he reached around her to open the door, and then held it for her to enter.

Grudgingly, Starr stepped through. "Have it your way. The sooner you show me whatever—whoever—it is, the sooner we can leave."

The bar was wreathed with plastic holly and twinkle lights and packed with people. Matt—presumably the real one—and several members of her team occupied one of the wooden booths. Judging from the empty glassware littering the tabletop and the slouched postures of everyone but him, they'd been here a while. Matt, she remembered from their office Fine Wine Fridays, wasn't much of a drinker.

She whipped around to the spirit. "They went to Central Bar?"

Expression inscrutable, he nodded. "Indeed, they did."

Until now, it hadn't occurred to her that the drinks meet-up might be in her hood, let alone just a five minutes' walk from her building. She'd been so intent on saying no to Matt that she hadn't thought to ask where they were headed. Who knew, if she'd agreed to come along, the evening might have ended with Matt, the *real* Matt, walking her home. The thought had her feeling fluttery—and wistful.

They edged closer to the table just as Terri slammed her beer mug on the top. "Seriously, Matt, are you like…

defending her? After what she's just done to us, all of us, how can you?"

Leaning into Spirit Matt, Starr whispered, "You're sure they can't see or hear us?"

Dividing her gaze between two Matts, the spirit version and the man, was disorienting to say the least. Even for someone who'd grown up on fantasies of alternate universes and time bends, it was a lot to wrap her mind around.

He nodded. "We're air to them."

Starr swallowed hard and returned her attention to the table.

Matt spoke up. "I'm just saying she's under a lot of pressure to put out the February issue, especially with Macie gone, and she could use our support."

Kent, the production assistant, scoffed. "Since when does the Iron Lady need anyone's support?"

Starr turned to Spirit Matt. "They call me the Iron Lady? Like Meryl Streep playing Margaret Thatcher in the movie?"

He shifted on his feet and stared down, much like the real Matt sometimes did when he was weighing his words—and trying not to hurt someone's feelings. "I suppose it could be interpreted as a compliment."

Sure the reference could be a compliment—only taking in the byplay, the smirking and elbowing and eye-rolling. but she didn't doubt it was meant as anything but a dig. "Yeah, well, I'm not running for political office. I don't need to be popular. I just need to get the freakin' magazine out and to do that I don't need friends. I need workhorses."

The spirit shushed her. "Quiet, you're missing it—and it's about to get really good."

Reluctantly, she turned back.

Terri—tongue loosened from several beers judging from the empty bottles parked in front of her—was taking no prisoners. "I guess we'll all be *supporting* her bright and early on December twenty-sixth. When I called my folks to tell them I'd have to drive back on Christmas night and miss our annual midnight walk on the beach, my mom cried. She fucking cried, Matt."

Jim, the production manager, traveled his bleary gaze about the group. "My twin brother's on leave from Afghanistan. I haven't seen Dave since he shipped out. We made a pact to spend the holiday week hanging out in Ohio, just the two of us. Now I'm not going to get to see him, not for Christmas, not at all!"

Scott, Starr's head copywriter and silent until now, added, "Look, Landry, I get that you're a nice guy and a team player, and I respect you, I do. But what you're not getting here— what's missing from the equation for you—is that Starling's not playing on any team but her own. Wake up and smell the coffee, man. We're nothing but slaves to her. *Slaves*."

Starr swallowed hard. That she'd just said as much to Spirit Matt wasn't lost on her. For the first time in a long time, she felt genuinely ashamed of her behavior. Knowing that she was hated, more or less universally, was hard enough to face. Knowing that she'd *earned* it, every snicker and sour word, made it doubly hard to stand her ground and watch.

She turned to Spirit Matt, but his attention was riveted on the scene ahead almost as if he'd forgotten her. Reaching out, she touched his elbow, solid beneath the glittery garb. "Can we go now—please?"

Still staring ahead, he shook his head. "Be patient. I told you it's about to get really good."

She forced herself to turn back. What more could they possibly say to wound her? She was half afraid to find out.

Real Matt pursed his lips—his beautifully shaped, kissable lips—and shook his head. "I don't think that's fair or true. Sure, she works the team hard but she works herself hardest of any of us."

He was defending her! When was the last time someone had had her back? Other than her mother, she couldn't think of a single soul.

"Yeah, well, unlike us, she managed to score a big fat holiday bonus for herself while we get nada. What about that?" Kent growled.

Starr had stood by silently—or mostly silent—until now, but enough was enough. "That is so not fair!"

She'd fought hard to get her people bonuses, damned hard, lion hard. Didn't they get that the final decision wasn't hers, but that of corporate? She couldn't help that magazine revenues were down or that the country was still stuck in an economic recession. Her own end-of-year bonus had been slashed by half from the previous year as part of the fallout she was still fielding from Macie's blown undercover investigation. Starr was the managing editor, as her boss had felt the need to point out at her annual performance review earlier that month. They were paying her to manage her people, not be their bestie. Starr had had no choice but to grit her teeth and take the lecture in silence and the check in hand. She had rent and bills to pay just like they did. What was she supposed to have done, give the money back?

A sly smile slipped over Kent's face. "Maybe you don't have to miss that beach walk with your family after all, Terri."

Matt whipped around to Kent. "What are you saying?"

Kent braced both elbows on the beer-sopped table and leaned closer. "What if we were to go rogue on her? Not in-your-face rogue like what Graham pulled. More like coming down with the Blue Flu."

The Blue Flu? They wouldn't dare...

Scott straightened. "We call in sick at the same time? You think that'll work?"

Kent shrugged. "What's she gonna do, fire us all? If she wants that precious February issue to make it out of the gate, she won't dare." His gaze glinted. "We'll have Boss Lady by the balls."

The girl from reception, nameless to Starr, giggled. "Brass balls, you mean."

Terri stopped tracing the water ringing the bottom of her glass and brightened. "That's genius!"

Starr sucked in a gasp. Didn't they understand what was at stake? If they blew February, the biggest revenue-generating issue of the year, the magazine would sink faster than the *Titanic* and then none of them, Starr included, would have jobs. She swung her gaze back to Matt. Even before he spoke, his expression told her that he alone understood.

He pushed back his chair and stood. "You all do what you want, but I'm going in on December twenty-sixth, and if I have to eat, shower, and sleep in the office all week to get the February issue out on time, I'll do it."

Kent's gaze narrowed. "What's your problem, Landry? Don't tell me, let me guess—bad bout of 'hot for teacher'?"

Kent never knew what hit him, not until it was too late. Matt launched himself across the bar table, grabbed the smirking photographer by the shirt collar, and, freeing up one fisted hand, socked him squarely in the jaw. Spit and blood sloshed out of the agape mouth. Standing tall like the Jedi knight of Starr's geek-girl fantasies, Matt let go and took a step back.

Bravado crumbling like a stale Christmas cookie, Kent slid back down into his booth seat, clutching his split lip. "Jesus, I think you loosened a tooth."

Matt flexed his hand, the knuckles already showing bruises. "If I did, you asked for it. Next time, it'll be a broken nose."

Seeing him, normally so mild-mannered and chill, lose control was shocking—and super sexy. Feeling as if her heart were swelling, Starr spun around to Spirit Matt. "Thank you!" She reached out to touch him but dropped her hand before she could, her emotions a tangle of awe, gratitude—and desire.

He snapped his fingers and the bar scene froze. "Don't thank me, thank him. I'm just a hallucination, remember?" The grin he gave her was the same she'd by now seen on countless occasions when, even in the midst of magazine mayhem, their gazes always seemed to meet and meld as if they were the only two people in the room.

Starr felt the corners of her own mouth lifting. So this was what smiling felt like. It had been so long she scarcely remembered. "Not a hallucination—a dream."

And maybe, just maybe, her Dream Man.

Chapter Five

Another dizzying *whoosh* carried them to their final stop: Christmas Future. Recalling Dickens's text—the slender volume had started out as a ghost story after all—Starr steeled herself. She had a pretty good idea of how this last visit would go—grim, definitely grim.

She opened her eyes and looked around. They were in Manhattan still, on the Upper East Side at 96th Street. The building before them looked to be about twenty stories, neither posh nor poor. They entered the modest lobby. A tidily dressed attendant kept vigil behind the desk. Out of habit, Starr stopped to sign in, and then remembered that she was, for the present purpose, invisible.

Spirit Matt led them over to the elevators. The doors opened and they stepped on.

"Traveling by elevator seems like a comedown after flying," she joked as the doors closed.

They stopped on the sixth floor and the spirit led the way down the modest, carpeted hallway. Two apartments flanked the far end. Starr started to ask which unit when the door to

6C flew open.

"This whole 'open sesame' thing, I'll never get used to it," she quipped, crossing the threshold to the inside.

"Fortunately you won't have to, not for many more years," he assured her, following her in.

So it seemed she had a long life ahead. That was both good and good to know. Tabling her curiosity, she looked around. Whoever lived here obviously loved them some Christmas. Fresh pine and cinnamon scented the air. Poking her head inside the small galley-style kitchen, Starr spotted the pot of wassail simmering on the stovetop—yum! From an unseen sound system, the legendary Nat King Cole crooned his Christmas classic. A black-and-white tuxedo cat raced by, batting about a Santa Claws catnip-stuffed toy.

"Molly Jane!" Starr snapped her gaze from the cat to the spirit. "What's my cat doing here? Did we move?"

Spirit Matt smiled knowingly. "Good question."

A large, beautifully decorated pine dominated the main room. Giggling drew her gaze beneath it. Curled up on a buffalo plaid blanket, the remains of a Christmas carpet picnic pushed to one side, her future self hung on Matt Landry like tinsel!

Starr whipped her head around to the spirit. "This is your—I mean, Matt's apartment?"

He nodded. "It is."

Her once dreaded holiday birthday was definitely looking up. Eager to see what might come next, Starr turned back to the couple beneath the tree.

Her future self looked up from the latest of the packages crowded around her. "So many gifts, Matt, you're spoiling me." The stunning smile she sent him so softened her face that Starr scarcely recognized it as her own.

He grinned. "That's my plan. Besides, it's not just Christmas, it's also your birthday. And I saved the big gift for last." He pushed a huge, gorgeously gift-wrapped box toward her.

Like an excited child, her future self tore through the paper and lifted the lid. Only the big box led to a slightly less big box. She unwrapped it only to find yet another box inside.

Looking up, she groaned. "You, Matthew Gabriel Landry, are total evil. How did I miss this before?"

He shrugged, a smile breaking over his face. "Better the devil you know…"

Six boxes and a mound of shed wrapping paper later, she came to the final small square box. Her future self hesitated, looking over at Matt. "Matt, is this what I think it is?"

Watching her future self with breath bated, Starr could scarcely contain herself. "Just open it, will you!"

"Open it and see," Future Matt echoed, an uncertain smile playing about his lips.

Starr held her breath as her future self lifted the hinged lid with shaking hands. Her head shot up. She held the box at arm's length. The midnight blue velvet lining set off the princess cut diamond to perfection.

"Oh…my…God! You got me a diamond ring, a diamond *engagement* ring!"

Matt smiled. "Well, I certainly hope it's an engagement ring. That was the plan, anyway. Like it?"

"Like it? Oh, Matt, I love it. I love you!"

Visibly relieved, he reached for her. "I love you, too, baby, but before we get too carried away, I've got to get this right." He shifted so that he was kneeling. Her future self followed suit. Facing her, he reached for her hand. "Cynthia Starling— Starr—will you make me the luckiest man alive by doing me the honor of becoming my wife?"

Her future self didn't hesitate. "Yes, yes, of course I will!"

Smiling, he slid the diamond onto her left ring finger. Carrying her hand to his mouth, he kissed the tops of her trembling fingers.

The scene unfolding before them represented Starr's most secret, heartfelt wish, a wish she'd never fully acknowledged—until now. Blinking misty eyes, she reached for Spirit Matt's hand. His fingers wrapped around hers, so warm and alive she could hardly believe he wasn't as flesh-and-blood real as the "shadows" they watched.

Beneath the tree, Future Matt brushed his mouth over Starr's, then trailed kisses over her jaw, her neck, and the tops of her Christmas sweater–covered breasts. Suddenly the tempo turned from sweet to seductive, the temperature ratcheting from warm to melting. Moaning, her future self reached around and lifted his T-shirt. Bringing it up over his arms and head, she tossed it boldly aside. Starr stared. Her future self stared. Feeling like a voyeur, she reminded herself that the erotic scene unfolding was hers, or at least her future. Voyeur or not, she couldn't drag her gaze away. She didn't *want* to drag her gaze away. Until now, she'd never seen Matt without a shirt. His broad shoulders, sculpted biceps, and flat six-pack stomach exceeded her hottest hopes.

Desire, at once raw and tender, suffused Matt's handsome face. "Oh, baby, I love you so much, I want you so bad." He eased her back onto the blanket and came down atop her.

Colored Christmas lights dappled his broad, sweat-slicked back, the sinewy flesh smooth and supple beneath her future self's stroking fingers, red-polished nails lightly scoring his skin. Watching him kiss and fondle and shape her shadow's form, Starr could almost feel the imprint of his mouth and hands and weight on her physical body, releasing a flood of pure joy and...*rightness.*

"We'll pause it at PG-13," Spirit Matt announced, his voice ever so slightly shaky.

The spirit snapped his fingers and the two figures froze. Staring at the sexy tableau, Starr focused on calming her pounding heart and reclaiming her stalled breathing. Matt Landry wanted her. More than wanted her, he loved her, powerfully loved her, or at least he would at some point in the not too far future. He didn't care that she was his boss. He didn't care that she made more money than he did. He didn't even care that she was seven years older. None of that mattered, not to him. Why had that mattered so very much to her? Sure, dating an office subordinate was frowned upon but there wasn't any actual policy against it. Had she seized on her age and seniority to rationalize keeping him away?

Spirit Matt turned to her, his expression concerned. "Are you okay?"

She faced him, simultaneously embarrassed and turned on. "Yeah, I'm...good. Great, I mean. It looks like everything's going to work out for...them—us."

His gaze dimmed. "I still have one more scene to show you."

She hesitated, scalp prickling. "But this is Christmas Future, the final stop, the end of the line." When he only regarded her with pressed-together lips, she felt panic build. "Look, I don't know about you or The Powers That Be, but I at least have read the actual Dickens text. Whatever film remake you're relying on, believe me, it's bogus."

He shook his head. "In your case, your future path is split. Think of it as a metaphysical fork in the road. Before you decide which way to go, there's an alternate Christmas Future you need to see."

Starr held up a hand. "That's really...conscientious of you, but I'm good with this version..." She glanced back at the intertwined lovers beneath the tree, her breath catching. "Really good. I don't need to see any more." A carpet picnic ending with smoking hot sex and an engagement ring—how could such a path possibly be improved upon?

Spirit Matt sent her an apologetic look. "Sorry, Starr, but

it's not up to me."

He took her hand without waiting for her to give it, their interlocked fingers levitating them instantly. As in her apartment earlier, the glass window lifted as if opened by invisible hands. Starr ducked as they soared out.

Once again they were flying over the city, the night air balmy despite the snow resuming. Gliding over the white marbled façade of Grand Central Station, clearing the peaks of the Chrysler and Empire State Buildings, they headed in the direction of downtown. Crossing over Delancey Street, they set down in the Lower East Side.

Staring up at the row of dilapidated buildings, Starr felt foreboding take hold. "Please tell me I don't live here in the future."

"Like so many things, that's up to you. You're the Boss Lady, after all."

"Don't call me that!" Starr snapped.

He drew back, feigning surprise. "But I thought you liked being the boss, always in the driver's seat, whipping the… workhorses into shape, breaking others down so you can build them back up—in your image."

Using her words against her—what a cheap shot! "Maybe I did, but I don't want that anymore, especially not if it leads to…this." She flung out a hand to the crumbling stone steps he seemed to be guiding her toward.

At his nod, she gave in and ascended on suddenly shaking legs. The hallway inside was low ceilinged and dank. A second set of short, slippery stairs led them down to the basement. Three apartment units occupied the lowest level. The spirit stepped forward and rang the buzzer for 1A.

From inside, a woman bellowed, "I'm coming. Keep your f-ing boxers on!"

The door opened. A bent old woman with thinning copper-and-white curls glared through them out into the hallway. Wrinkled face twisted in a scowl, she took a step out.

"Freakin' brats, ringing my bell and running off, I'll call the heat on you next time, see if I don't." Giving her moth-eaten sweater a tug, she marched out into the hallway.

Starr's gaze followed her. *No, it can't be!*

Sidestepping the shadow, the spirit gestured for Starr to follow him inside. Distracted with watching the old woman depart, she nearly missed his cue. She cleared the threshold and the apartment door slammed. Caught off guard, she started.

"Someone's jumpy," Spirit Matt observed.

Starr looked over her shoulder. "I'm not jumpy, I'm concerned. Won't she be locked out?"

He shook his head. "She wears the key on a chain around her neck. But why should you care if some old woman spends the night out in the cold?"

Starr opened her mouth to answer him but instead found herself fighting the urge to gag. Dirty cat dishes and litter pans were scattered about on the soiled carpeting. The acrid odor of cat urine stung her nose and made her eyes water. Cats of various colors, sizes, and breeds roamed, climbing the sagging bookshelves and counters, scaling the tattered sofa back, and leaping from one stack of old magazines to the next. Curious, she walked over to check out one of the piles. Pulling an age-yellowed publication off, she held it up to the oily light. The cover bore a modified version of the *On Top* logo.

Oh, God! The cursing crone *was* her! She'd joked often enough about one day becoming a cranky cat lady, but faced with that scenario now, her possible future was no laughing matter.

Prepared to plead, she shot her gaze to the spirit. "Please, please tell me this isn't my future."

He followed her over, gently prying the periodical from

her hand. "That, Starr, is entirely up to you."

Unlike the scenes from Christmas Past and Present, her Christmas Future was still a wild card. Cranky old woman with too many cats or blissful bride making love with her hunky husband-to-be, she didn't have to stop and ask herself which scenario she wanted to come true. The choice, such as it was, was clear as glass. What remained unanswered was how to influence it.

Raspy voiced, she finally asked, "But you're showing me this…place because it's at least a…possibility, right?"

He nodded. "It is, as possible as the previous future scenario."

She scraped a hand through her hair, thankfully still thick and lustrous. "Can you give me some odds here? Can we poll The Powers That Be at least?"

He smiled. "The Powers That Be aren't one of your beta testing groups."

"Sorry, right, but back to those odds, a percentage maybe?"

He blew out a breath. "Okay, fifty-fifty."

Wow, her fate was split straight down the middle? He was right—this was definitely not one of her consumer testing groups. Their feedback ratings were usually all over the board.

"What's the wild card, the tipping point, the influencing variable?" she prodded.

His face wore a look of strained patience. "Isn't it obvious?"

"I'm guessing we don't have much time left, so just tell me, for crap's sake."

Spirit Matt let out a long sigh. "The wild card, the tipping point, the influencer is *you*."

Chapter Six

"Matt, come back! *Matt*!"

Screaming, Starr awoke. She was in her apartment on the sofa where she'd first fallen asleep. A lightening gray sky showed through her window. The shoebox was still beneath her coffee table, Molly Jane now wrapped around it. Everything looked the same. Everything *was* the same — everything except her. Now that she was calming, she realized that inside she felt enormously, wonderfully...*different*.

Giddy with a newfound feeling of freedom and tingling from head to toe with a previously unknown sense of joy, she reached for her cell phone lying on the coffee table. Though she'd forgotten to charge it, she still had one bar left. Opening her contacts list, she typed the first few letters of the name for which she searched—Macie. Drawing a deep breath, she hit send on the call. A groggy voice answered on the fourth ring.

"Macie, it's me, Starr... Yeah I know it's kind of early... Five o'clock in the morning? Seriously? Shit, sorry about that. Listen, I won't keep you. I just wanted to say thanks for the shoes and for remembering my birthday and, well,

I'm sorry I didn't make the wedding, but I hope you'll let me know when you're in New York next, and bring the husband and the kid, too… Yes, really. I mean, why not? The more the merrier. Oh, and if you need or even just want me to write you a recommendation or whatever, you've got it… No, I'm not drunk. Well, I did have one beer last night but that was it. Okay, so I'll let you get back to the whole newlywed first Christmas together thing, and we'll catch up after the New Year. For now, Merry Christmas, Mace. Ciao."

Ending the call, she scrolled through her saved e-mail messages, found the invitation to the Matzo Ball Pot Luck Supper to be held that night at her assistant editor Terri's Brooklyn Heights apartment, and changed her RSVP from "no" to "yes."

Bursting with energy, she leapt up, threw on her coat and boots, and dashed out to the nearest ATM. Crossing Union Square Park to the bank, her boot soles making music on the frozen ground, she smiled up at the lightening sky.

"Thank you, Powers That Be. Thank you, Spirit Matt. I won't waste this chance or this Christmas—or any Christmas—ever again, I swear it!"

Back in her apartment, she spent the morning purging her closet and dresser of designer clothes and accessories and makeup samples. Bagging it all up, she showered and dressed, then headed to the homeless shelter in Astor Place.

She found Jimmie—AKA Santa Claus—ensconced in an improvised throne in the center's event room. Balancing twin boys on either knee, his eyes popped when he saw her. She waited for him to finish taking the kids' Christmas orders before approaching.

He leapt up from his seat. "Ms. S., you made it!"

"I almost didn't," she admitted.

He looked down at the shopping bags dangling from both her hands. "Wow, that's a lot of stuff you've got. Looks like you'll be giving me a run for my money as Santa."

Starr set the bags down. "I don't know about that, but I'd really like to take you up on your offer to help out with serving the dinner...if I'm still welcome." For the first time since awakening back in her apartment, she felt her confidence flag.

"Of course you're welcome. We'll go find my wife, Nancy, and have her show you around."

Feeling shy, Starr hesitated. "Before you do, I have something for you, your Christmas bonus. I should have given it to you yesterday but... Well, Merry Christmas." She slipped the envelope from her purse and handed it to him.

Beaming, he took it. "That's so nice of you to come all this way to give it to me. Thanks! You're the best, Ms. S."

Starr hesitated. She hadn't been the best or anything close to it, but from here on that would change. "There's something else I hope you'll accept, my apology."

Expression blank, he stared at her. "What for?"

"I was rude to you yesterday, rude and out of line. The truth is, I was dreading today being Christmas, and I took it out on you. I hope you'll forgive me—and most of all, I hope you'll put me to work!"

He grinned and tucked the envelope inside his Santa suit. "No worries, Ms. S., Christmas makes a lot of people bat shit. I figure it's my job to keep the mood upbeat, to make sure you and the other tenants always walk in to a smile—and a joke if you're up for it. Now let's go find my Nancy and she can get you started."

Before they could take more than a few steps toward the door, a slender brunette wearing a worried look and a Mrs. Claus apron approached.

"There's Nancy now." Jimmie held up his arm and hailed her over. "Hey, hon, there's someone I want you to meet. This is one of the tenants from my building, Cynthia Starling."

Joining them, Jimmie's wife's gentle gaze brushed over her. "You must be the Ms. S. Jimmie's always talking about."

Starr girded herself. God only knew what tales Jimmie had carried home, not that she blamed him. She hadn't always been the most appreciative tenant, usually in too much of a rush to do more than nod in passing. Certainly she hadn't hung around to hear any jokes.

"Yes, that's me, only please call me Starr."

"Nice to meet you, Starr. Jimmie's always going on about how nice everyone is in *his* building." She flashed a smile and then turned back to her husband with a sigh. "We have a frozen food situation. The volunteer in charge of kitchen prep last night forgot to take the turkeys out of the freezer to thaw. It looks like Christmas lunch is going to be Christmas dinner for sure. Any ideas on how I can fill up the time? You've got the kids covered with activities, but what do I do about the moms?"

Listening, Starr looked down to one of her shopping bags, bulging with never opened cosmetic samples and beauty supplies and inspiration struck. "I think I may have an answer."

"Makeovers, that's a great idea!" Nancy assured her almost as soon as the suggestion was out.

Within twenty minutes, Starr found herself amidst nearly fifty women of all ages, shapes, and ethnicities lined up. The room buzzed with excitement. Santa Jimmie led the kids off to the dining hall to learn to make a gingerbread house. Starr set to work, quickly transforming the event room into a makeshift day spa. At the end of the afternoon, each woman left to sit down to Christmas dinner with a bright, smiling face and a goody bag of beauty samples.

Watching them go off, heads held high and shoulders pulled back, Starr had a sense of satisfaction beyond anything she'd felt from putting out a year of magazines. Pleasantly weary, she briefly considered calling it a day and going home. But spending yet another Christmas evening home alone seemed both anticlimactic and a serious step back. After the previous night's "dream," she knew the grim end to which that led.

Brooklyn Heights was something of a trek, especially as the subway was running on a delayed holiday schedule, but the extended travel gave her a chance to collect her courage. By the time she made it to Terri's building—a turn-of-the-century brownstone subdivided into apartments—her main anxiety was that everyone might have left. Chatter and music from within set that fear to rest. Standing outside in the hallway, she pulled off her snow-dampened boots, set them beside the welcome mat, and took out the box of what she'd come to think of as her Cinderella slippers. Holding one hand against the wall to balance herself, she slipped on the heels.

Excited and nervous, she put the shoebox back in her bag and reached out to ring the buzzer. The door opened. Matt stood framed within. Her heart somersaulted. She'd supposed—okay, hoped—he'd be here and yet…

Stunned, she blurted out the first stupid thought that sprang to mind. "I didn't know you were Jewish." The annual holiday dinner for Jewish singles was typically held on Christmas Eve, not Christmas, but of course she'd kept everyone working too late the night before for that.

"I'm not," he admitted. "I just thought it sounded like something fun to do, since I don't have time to fly home to my folks."

He said the latter as a straightforward statement-of-fact, no barbed look or tone of recrimination, but still she winced, remembering the bar scene from her "dream."

"About that—"

"Whoa, you've got some serious footwear going on." His gaze glided over her, a big grin breaking over his face as he settled on her feet. "I don't think I've ever seen you wear anything other than boots."

Starr flexed her foot, the motion showing off the shoes' twinkling. "They're vintage Saks. They were a gift from a friend. A *female* friend," she added, wanting to be broadcast clear about her status as single and available. "Actually, Macie mailed them."

Was it her imagination or did his shoulders relax? "That's great you two are mending fences. Anyway, come in."

Peering around him, she saw the party was in full force with about a dozen guests packed into the slender space, including everyone who'd appeared in her "dream's" Christmas Present at Central Bar. Talk about stepping inside a lions' den. Courage waning, she held back.

"Matt, who is it?" Terri called from inside.

"It's Starr," he answered.

Shit, no turning back now. Crossing the threshold, Starr didn't miss how conversations suddenly ceased as she entered.

"Happy Hanukkah," she called out to the quieting room.

Her assistant editor approached carrying a cake platter. "Thanks," Terri said, expression uncertain. "Glad you could make it."

Starr girded herself to get the tough stuff out of the way first. "Listen up, people. About the holiday leave, I've decided the all-hands meeting can wait until Monday morning. I'm giving you the rest of the week off—with pay."

Gazes widened and jaws fell, Matt's included. "Seriously? That's really generous of you."

"But what about the print production deadline?" someone asked.

Starr didn't flinch. The word—deadline—had controlled her for far too long as it was. "At least half of our subscribers read us digitally anyway. Maybe being late going to the stands will encourage more people to go green."

Hand fisted about a beer, Kent shouldered his way toward her. "What's the catch?"

Starr didn't miss how Matt moved closer. Warmed by the protective gesture, she shook her head. "No catch," she confirmed, keeping her cool. "Consider it my way, my *new* way, of saying happy holidays."

"So what do you think of Terri's cake?" Matt prompted.

For the first time since arriving, Starr took an actual look at the platter Terri held. A star-shaped sheet cake sat atop it. Frosted in Christmas red and green, it read, "May All Your Christmas Birthdays be Starr Bright."

Starr's gaze flew from the cake to Terri and finally to Matt. "How did you—"

"Happy Christmas Birthday!"

Matt, Terri, indeed everyone looked to Starr as though expecting her to shove the cake in Terri's face, storm out, or something equally shitty. Instead she did something guaranteed to floor them all. She smiled.

"Butter cream—my favorite!" she exclaimed, daring to dip a finger into the cake's side. Tasting her frosting-covered fingertip, she said, "God, that's good." She turned back to Terri. "You...made this?"

Terri nodded. "I have a cake-baking business on the side—nothing that interferes with my work at the magazine," she added quickly. "I just bake for a few events a month—bar mitzvahs, anniversaries, and um...birthdays."

"You're really talented," Starr said sincerely, recalling the spirit's advice on giving compliments. In the past, both her management and personal style had been based on breaking people down. Going forward, she would focus on lifting them up. "Any chance you do Valentine's Day cakes as well?"

Terri hesitated. "Sure, I mean, I could."

"Perfect. Why don't you bake another cake, think Cupid and hearts and flowers, and bring it into work on Monday.

We'll run it in February's Sweet Treats sidebar."

Terri's gaze looked poised to pop. "You'd actually promote my baking business in the magazine?"

Starr shrugged. "You'll be doing me a favor. We're short on copy for the food column. I guess being behind schedule has perks after all." She turned back to a beaming Matt. "You know a food photographer who's good with cakes?"

"My food guy's still on vacation, but I'll shoot it myself."

"Great." She dragged her gaze away and turned back to Terri, whose mouth was hanging at half-mast. "That work for you?"

"That sounds…awesome."

Feeling what might just be tears forming, Starr summoned her usual briskness. "It's settled then. Now, let's get this birthday party started."

A chorus of "Happy Birthday" threatened to rock the roof, followed by a toast in her honor. Tears welled and this time there was no mistaking the sensation. Dashing them away, Starr traveled her gaze along the table. Saving the best for last, she lingered on Matt. He'd kept to her side since she'd arrived.

"Speech, speech!" someone, and then everyone, chanted.

Starr took a moment to clear the knot of emotion from her throat before beginning. "I don't know what to say other than thank you from the bottom of my heart—and yes, I do have one." There was a pause and then nervous laughter followed. "I'm not exactly sure how to put this, but let's just say things at the magazine are going to start changing in a big way—for the better."

A hush descended. Faces fell. A groan could be heard from the room's back. God, did they think she meant layoffs? Even Matt tensed beside her as though bracing for bad news.

She raced on to reassure them. "That memo about no holiday bonuses this year, well that was just a corporate screw up." She reached into her shoulder bag for the stack of rubber-banded gift cards. "It's not as much as I'd like it to be, for sure it's not as much as you all deserve, but I hope you'll accept it in the spirit in which it's given—in the spirit of…Christmas."

She'd deposit her bonus check from the magazine tomorrow, but fortunately she'd had sufficient funds in her account to cover getting the gift cards in advance. It didn't feel fair to keep the money, not while all the people on her team who'd made her look good—who'd made her successful—did without. Two hundred dollars per person wouldn't change anyone's life, but if it bought someone and their spouse a lovely New Year's Eve out or helped buy a coveted toy for their kid, then it was…*something.*

She handed the stack to Terri to hand out and headed into the hallway under the pretense of needing some air. Screw pretense, her face felt warm and her limbs shaky. Being the focus for curses and glares was one thing. Being center stage in bringing joy—in making people *smile*—was unchartered territory.

Footsteps followed her out. The door creaked closed and Matt stepped into the hallway. "That was your bonus money, wasn't it?" He held out the white gift card envelope on which his name was scrawled in her less than neat handwriting.

She answered with a shrug. "Me give away money? What have you been smoking, Landry?"

He rolled his eyes. "I don't smoke weed or cigarettes, and I'm pretty sure you know that. And stop calling me Landry. I really hate it."

Spirit Matt had said the same last night. "Fair enough… Matt."

"Better, thanks. By the way, how was your Christmas Eve?"

Starr hesitated. "It was… good. I picked up some Thai food and fell asleep on the couch watching an old black-and-white version of...*A Christmas Carol*. You know, just a nice quiet holiday at home," she added, hiding a smile.

"Sounds nice," he said. "Maybe I should have come over instead of going to the bar," he added, gaze holding hers.

Starr hesitated, moistening her suddenly dry lips. "Maybe I should have invited you."

"Maybe you should have," he said, taking a step closer. "I might have slept better."

Startled, she asked, "You didn't sleep?"

He shrugged. "I did, but I had weird dreams."

Fishing, she asked, "What about?"

He looked away, but not before she caught the color climbing his neck. "I don't know, like I said, it was messed up. Mostly it was about Christmas, not this Christmas, but other Christmases in the past and...future. I was me but not really me, and you were there and we were doing a lot of flying around the city and other crazy crap."

Recalling the vivid scene of them together in the future—the carpet picnic beneath the Christmas tree, his poignant proposal, and last but not least, how amazing he'd looked shirtless—sent her temperature spiking and her heart hammering. Had they met up in some alternate universe and shared the same Christmas Eve "dream"? Was that even possible? What was for sure possible was they were together here and now.

"Crazy crap, huh?" she said, feeling a no doubt silly grin spreading over her face. All this smiling was making the muscles in her face hurt...not that she was planning on stopping.

"And flying," he reminded her, grinning back.

He shoved the gift card in his jeans' front pocket, and for the first time she spotted his swollen knuckles. Defending her honor by clocking Kent, had that actually...*happened*? She opened her mouth to ask but before she could, he cut her off.

"So now that Christmas is just about over, I guess the next big holiday to gear up for is New Year's."

Wondering where he might be leading, she nodded. "Yeah, I guess it is."

He closed the space between them with a single stride. "I was hoping you'd be my date for New Year's Eve." His big, warm hands took gentle hold of her shoulders.

She felt her mouth fall open. He wasn't only asking her out. He was asking her out for freakin' New Year's Eve!

What to Wear (and NOT to Wear) to Sleigh Him on New Year's Eve. She'd written off the copy as a typical holiday fluff piece, but now she had to fight the urge to race home and read every word.

He stroked her arms, raising a trail of delicious shivers there and everywhere else. "You still haven't answered me."

"It's uh…really hard to…think with you doing that."

He stood his ground. "Good. You think too much as it is."

"I do?"

He nodded. "You talk a lot too, not that I mind—*usually.*" He flashed a smile. "But back to our New Year's date—I'm thinking we'll start with dinner, some place intimate and kind of quiet, at least as quiet as it gets on New Year's Eve, and then afterward some friends of mine are having a party at their place. Not a party really, just a few couples over to drink champagne and watch the ball drop on TV. But if you already have plans, I'll—"

"I'd love to," she blurted out, heart pounding.

"Great, I'll swing by your building and pick you up. Eight o'clock, okay?"

"Perfect," she said. "I'll text you my address."

He hesitated, a sheepish look taking over his face. "I, uh…already have it?"

"You do?"

He hesitated. "The first rule of any new job: make friends with someone in HR."

"You have a mole in Human Resources!" Giving out confidential employee information to another employee was so against the rules! She should go ballistic, demand he give up his source, but before she could do either, it struck her. "That's how everyone knew Christmas was my birthday. You told them!"

He didn't deny it. "I've been at *On Top* for six months now and it seems like there's a birthday celebrated about once a week, but so far not yours. I figured it had to be coming around soon. I never figured you for a Christmas baby, though. Saint Patrick's Day maybe, but not Christmas." He reached out and fingered one copper-colored curl.

Shivering, she managed a shaky laugh. "Yeah, I look like my mother screwed one of the Keebler elves or Chuckie."

He shook his head, looking at her as though she was a lost cause he was determined to redeem. "You're beautiful." He cradled her face gently between his two hands, as if her pale skin were made of porcelain indeed. "You're more than beautiful. You're perfect."

The dream scene from Christmas Future flashed through her thoughts and she felt herself blushing. "I guess having an HR mole means you know my birth year, too?" It wasn't really a question, but she braced for his answer anyway.

"Yeah, I guess I do...*Cynthia*—or do you prefer Cindy?" He grinned wickedly.

"Let's just stick to Starr, okay? You don't mind...about the age difference, I mean?" She bit her lower lip, belatedly remembering she wore lipstick—oops!

He looked at her incredulously. "If anything, it makes you even sexier to me."

"You think I'm...sexy?" It might sound like she was fishing for compliments, but she wasn't. She'd thought of herself as cute, mildly attractive even, but sexy? Really, this was news.

His gaze turned steamy, the irises huge and black. "Oh, yeah, I do. Not just sexy—hot. I'll show you sometime soon, but for right now, take a step back."

"Step back?" Wondering what he had in mind, she let him back them to the doorway.

He smiled. "Great, stop. Perfect. Now look up."

Starr did—and suddenly she got it. Lowering her gaze to his face, melting in the heat burning from his eyes, she asked, "Is that what I think it is?"

"If you're thinking mistletoe, then yes."

She laughed. "Who hangs mistletoe at a Matzo Ball supper?"

"New York's a melting pot, so deal with it." Leaning closer, he reached out and lifted her chin on the edge of his hand. "For now, just kiss me."

He lowered his head and matched his mouth to hers. Starr sighed and sank against him. He tasted of butter cream and peppermint schnapps—the perfect Christmas confection. The touch of his tongue to hers shot an arrow of warmth straight down her spine. Inside her Cinderella slippers, her toes tingled.

He broke the kiss and drew back to look at her, his eyes twinkling like the stars she and the spirit had sped past in her "dream." "Merry Christmas Birthday, Starr."

"Merry Christmas, Matt."

He leaned in and Starr tipped her face up to meet him. This time when his mouth met hers, his kiss held the promise of all the many merry Christmas birthdays yet to come.

Acknowledgments

My heartfelt thanks and warm holiday wishes to my editors, Stacy Abrams and Alycia Tornetta, to my agent Louise Fury, and to Danielle, Jessica, Barbara, Sara, and everyone on my Entangled publicity team who've contributed their tremendous time, talent, and energy to making my Suddenly Cinderella Series such a success.

Last but never least, to the real Molly Jane AKA Jane for filling my days with braying meows, drooling kitty kisses and unconditional love for these past twelve years—and counting. Thanks for letting me "rescue" you, sweetie!

About the Author

Award-winning author Hope Tarr earned a Master's Degree in Psychology and a PhD in Education before facing the hard truth: she wasn't interested in analyzing people or teaching them. What she really wanted was to write about them! To date, Hope has written twenty historical and contemporary romance novels for multiple publishers including *Operation Cinderella*, the launch of her Suddenly Cinderella contemporary series for Entangled Publishing and *A Cinderella Christmas Carol,* the series' only novella. Hope is also a co-founder and current principal of Lady Jane's Salon™, New York City's first and only monthly romance reading series, now in its fourth year with satellite salons nationwide. Look for additional Suddenly Cinderella books continuing with Francesca's story in *Project Cinderella* and find Hope online at her websites at www.HopeTarr.com and www.LadyJaneSalonNYC.com as well as on Twitter (@ HopeTarr) and Facebook.

Discover more romance titles from Indulgence…

REFORMING THE CEO
a *South Beach* novel by Marisa Cleveland

Reece Rowe's going to get a taste of what she's been missing and heads to hot Vincent Ferguson's office to find out what the women in South Beach already seem to know about him. CEO Vin Ferguson has to improve his image with his financial backers, and his friends suggest dating a respectable woman. Ridiculous. Because delectable but snooty socialites like Reece are out of his league. But he can't believe what she just proposed…

THE REVENGE GAME
a *Players' Pact* novel by Alice Gaines

Nicole Westmore was my first love. The summer I worked for her father was the best time of my life…until he drove me away. And so, I decided to get even, opening rival hotels, slowly driving them out of business. Nicole is still running the company that's about to collapse and all my hard work will soon pay off. And then I catch sight of her at a wedding, and all those feelings come rushing back—for both of us. Still, she doesn't know what I've done—yet. What will one night in her bed hurt? Then I get up the next morning…and realize I've been kidnapped!

CATCHING THE CEO
a *Billionaire's Second Chance* novel by Victoria Davies

Billionaire Damien Reid can barely believe it when Caitlyn Brooks shows up at the conference reception. He has no desire to spend a moment longer with the infuriating woman than he has to. Except he can't seem to stop his eyes from following her or the unnerving need to ruffle her perfect feathers. When teasing turns to touching, he's not sure if it's the best or worst mistake of his life.

www.ingramcontent.com/pod-product-compliance
Lightning Source LLC
Chambersburg PA
CBHW022052170626
46808CB00003B/1451